Fairy Tales

Stories retold by
Maureen Spurgeon

Brown Watson
ENGLAND

GOLDILOCKS
and the Three Bears

There was once a girl whose hair was so pretty, long, fair and curly, that everyone called her Goldilocks.

Goldilocks and her family lived in a cottage at the edge of a great, big forest, and there was nothing she liked better than going for long walks on her own.

Goldilocks thought she must know every inch of that forest until, one morning, after she had set off a little earlier than usual, she saw something which gave her ...prise...

It was a little cottage she had never seen
before, with lace curtains at the windows and
smoke coming out of the chimney.

"Who can live here?" wondered
Goldilocks, and she knocked at the door.

She knocked at the door and waited. There was no answer. She knocked again. Still, no answer.

"Anyone at home?" she called, and knocked again, a little harder this time. The door creaked open.

Goldilocks stepped inside and looked all round such a cosy, little room. A fire burned cheerfully, and on the hob were three bowls of porridge – a big bowl, a smaller bowl, and a tiny, little bowl...

"I wonder who lives here?" thought Goldilocks again, never guessing it was the home of three bears – Daddy Bear, Mummy Bear and Baby Bear. She only knew how good that porridge looked on a fresh, spring morning.

She tasted Daddy Bear's porridge. That was too hot. Then, she tried Mummy Bear's porridge. That was too cold. But when she tasted Baby Bear's porridge, it was so good that Goldilocks soon ate it all up!

After eating all that porridge, Goldilocks wanted to sit down. So she tried Daddy Bear's chair. That was too hard. Then she tried Mummy Bear's chair, but that was too soft. Then, she tried Baby Bear's chair...

And that was just right! In fact, Goldilocks had never sat in such a comfortable chair! She wriggled and squirmed so much, that, in the end, the chair broke, and Goldilocks fell to the floor!

"Ooh!" she groaned. "I think I'd better go and lie down." So, she went upstairs.

And in the bedroom were three beds – Daddy Bear's bed, Mummy Bear's bed, and Baby Bear's bed…

First, she tried Daddy Bear's bed. But that was too hard. Then she tried Mummy Bear's bed. That was too soft. But Baby Bear's bed was so warm and so cosy that Goldilocks snuggled down and was soon fast asleep!

By this time, Daddy Bear, Mummy Bear and Baby Bear were coming back from their walk. They had only gone to the end of the forest path and back – "Just to let the porridge cool down," Mummy Bear had said.

"Who's been eating my porridge?" growled Daddy Bear.

"Who's been eating my porridge?" said Mummy Bear.

"Who's been eating my porridge?" cried Baby Bear. "There's none left!"

"And who's been sitting in my chair?"
roared Daddy Bear.

"Who's been sitting in my chair?" cried
Mummy Bear.

"Who's been sitting in my chair?" wailed
Baby Bear. "It's all broken!"

They went upstairs. "Who's been sleeping in my bed?" said Daddy Bear.

"Who's been sleeping in my bed?" squealed Mummy Bear.

"Who's been sleeping in my bed?" said Baby Bear, with a loud sob.

His cries woke Goldilocks and she sat straight up in bed. She could not believe her eyes when she saw three furry faces looking at her! "B-bears!" she blurted out, very frightened. "Th-three b-bears!"

Had Goldilocks known it, Daddy, Mummy and Baby Bear were gentle, kind bears. When they saw it was only a little girl who had been in their cottage, they were not nearly so angry as they might have been.

But Goldilocks only knew that she had to leave their cottage just as soon as she could. So she let out a scream, the loudest, longest scream she had ever screamed, making the three bears jump back at once!

This was Goldilocks' chance! She flung back the bedclothes and rushed out of the door and down the stairs, away back into the forest before the three bears knew what was happening!

On and on she ran through the forest until she felt she could run no more.

It seemed a long, long time before she reached the path to her own home. And there was her mother, waiting

anxiously at the gate. Goldilocks was so glad to see her.

"Where have you been, Goldilocks?" she cried. "Daddy was just going out to look for you!"

And so began the story of Goldilocks and the Three Bears.

"You naughty girl!" scolded her mother. "Haven't I always told you never to go inside strange places?"

"Goldilocks," said her daddy, "are you sure this tale about the three bears isn't an excuse because you do not know the forest as well as you thought?"

"No, Daddy!" cried Goldilocks.

"Here," she went on, taking his hand, "I'll take you to their cottage, myself. Then you'll see."

And she led the way back into the forest without stopping once, seeming sure of every step.

That was the first of many times Goldilocks
went back to the forest. But, no matter how
hard she searched, she did not find that little
cottage, nor the three bears – Daddy Bear,
Mummy Bear and Baby Bear.

PINOCCHIO

Geppetto was a poor toymaker whose dearest wish had always been to have a son. One day, as he sat at his work-bench making a wooden puppet, it seemed to look at him and to smile. "How I wish I could look on the face of my son," he said. "I would call him Pinocchio."

Geppetto did not know it, but the Blue Fairy had heard what he said.

"He deserves to have his wish granted," she thought. "Pinocchio shall be a son to Geppetto."

And, as Pinocchio's eyes opened wide, so there came a chirruping noise from the fireplace. "Meet Jiminy Cricket!" said the fairy. "He is your conscience to tell you right from wrong, Pinocchio."

Geppetto was overjoyed to have a son at last!
"You must go to school, Pinocchio," he said.
"That's right!" nodded Jiminy Cricket.
"Otherwise, you'll turn into a donkey."

Geppetto even sold his only jacket so that he could buy Pinocchio the spelling book he needed to take to school.

"Goodbye, Father!" he called. "I shall make you proud of me."

But that was before Pinocchio knew Fire-Eater's Puppet Theatre was in town! Taking no notice of Jiminy Cricket, he sold his book to buy a ticket – and soon he was on stage, singing and dancing.

Fire-Eater wanted Pinocchio to stay. But when the time came to move far away from home and Geppetto, he was afraid. Being a wonderful singing, dancing puppet didn't seem so clever, after all...

"Geppetto sold his jacket to send me to school," he sobbed to Jiminy Cricket. "He'll wonder where I am!"

Luckily for him, Fire-Eater knew Geppetto and he gave Pinocchio five pieces of gold to take home to him!

"I can buy Geppetto a new jacket," cried Pinocchio. "Five gold pieces!"

"Is that all?" scoffed a cat.

"Bury them in our magic field," said the fox with him. "You'll have a tree of gold next day!"

"No, Pinocchio!" said Jiminy Cricket. "That's Geppetto's money!"

How Pinocchio wished he had listened to Jiminy when he discovered that the crafty cat and the sly fox had dug up the gold he had buried!

The fairy heard Pinocchio crying and asked him what was wrong.

"I dropped the gold I was taking home to Geppetto," he sobbed. "Now I can't find it!" And as he spoke, something very strange happened...

Pinocchio's nose began to grow!
"Where do you think you lost the money?" asked the fairy.
"On the way to school," he cried. "It must have fallen out of my pocket."

By now, his nose was so long, he could hardly see the end of it!

"Well, Pinocchio," laughed the Blue Fairy, "now you know how one small lie can grow into a big lie – just like your nose!"

At once, Pinocchio promised not to tell any more lies, sobbing so hard that the fairy took pity on him. "If you had listened to Jiminy Cricket," she said, "none of this would have happened!"

Pinocchio knew this was true, and, full of good intentions, he set off home. He had only gone a little way when a carriage full of children came along, pulled by some very strange-looking donkeys!

"Come to the Land of Toys!" they cried. "Play all year round!"

"Don't listen to them," warned Jiminy Cricket. But Pinocchio was already jumping up, determined not to miss any of the fun.

He thought the Land of Toys was wonderful! No books, no lessons – just as much play as anyone wanted!

After a while, he noticed his ears felt rather heavy – heavy and long, thick and furry...

"I said that you'd turn into a donkey if you didn't go to school," scolded Jiminy Cricket. "What will you do now?"

"Geppetto!" cried Pinocchio. "I want to go home to Geppetto!"

Pinocchio was afraid everyone would laugh at his donkey ears. But the people were too upset even to notice. "Geppetto went to sea looking for you," they said. "We think he was swallowed by a whale!"

"Poor Father," cried Pinocchio. "I must find him!" He made his way to the place where Geppetto was last seen and jumped into the inky blackness of the sea, gusts of wind hitting him in the face.

Suddenly, he saw a light ahead. He swam towards it and found himself crawling, then walking into a sort of underground cavern. "Pinocchio!" cried a voice. "Pinocchio, my dear, brave son!"

Pinocchio had never been so glad to see anyone – even if he had swum inside a whale by mistake!

"We'll get through the whale's mouth, then make for the shore," he told Geppetto. "Just follow me!"

When the whale opened its mouth, they were out! But Pinocchio was soon very tired, swimming for Geppetto as well as himself. By the time Jiminy Cricket had guided them to dry land, he could hardly move.

The Blue Fairy was waiting when Geppetto carried him to dry land.

"Well done, Pinocchio," she said. "You have shown that you are a brave and loving son. You shall have your reward!"

And instead of a wooden puppet, Pinocchio became a real boy with a beaming smile for Geppetto – and a conscience of his own to tell him right from wrong. How happy Jiminy Cricket was for both his friends!

RED RIDING HOOD

There was once a girl called Little Red Riding Hood. That was not really her name, but her grandmother had made her a red hood and cape, rather like those which ladies wore under their hats when they went out riding. And so, Red Riding Hood was what everyone called her.

Now, Red Riding Hood was a nice little girl, always cheerful and kind. So, when she heard that her Grandma was ill, she asked if there was anything she could do to help.

"Well, Red Riding Hood," said her mother, "I'd be glad if you could take some food to Grandma and see how she is. But it would mean you'd have to go through the wood!"

"Oh, I don't mind!" cried Red Riding Hood. She was thinking how nice it would be to stroll through the wood, and maybe pick some flowers for Grandma on the way.

"Well," said her mother again, "you must promise to go straight to her house, and no dawdling! Remember not to stop and speak to anyone you don't know!"

Now, Red Riding Hood really did mean to do what she had been told. But it was all too easy to forget, especially with the sun shining and so much to see on the way.

It was all so quiet, she had no idea that anyone else was there.

"Little Red Riding Hood..." murmured the wolf, seeing the red cloak. "She'd make a fine supper..."

"Good day, Red Riding Hood," he said
with a friendly bow. "May I ask where you
are going?"

"To Grandma's cottage," she said. "On
the other side of the wood."

This set the wolf thinking.

"Why not take a short cut along this path, my dear?" he said, knowing very well that the way he pointed was twice as long...

But his idea was to get to the cottage long before Red Riding Hood. Then, he thought, he could eat up poor Grandma, as well. What a feast he would have!

Still panting a little, the wolf knocked on Grandma's door.

"Who is there?" she quavered.

"It's me, Grandma," replied the wolf, in a voice as sweet as he could make it. "Red Riding Hood."

"Red Riding Hood!" cried Grandma in delight. "Lift up the latch and come right in." And, with a loud roar, that wicked wolf burst into the cottage!

Poor Grandma fainted at once, but before the wolf could take the first bite, he heard the sound of a gun outside. Best put the old woman in the wardrobe, he decided.

The sound of guns told the wolf that hunters were about, and the wolf did not like hunters one bit! Besides, he thought, Red Riding Hood would be arriving soon...

So he put on Grandma's nightcap and gown and got into bed. Soon, a voice called, "Grandma! It's Red Riding Hood!"

"Come in, dear!" cried the wolf.

"Oh, Grandma!" exclaimed Red Riding Hood, as she came up to the bed. "What big eyes you have!"

"All the better to see you with!" murmured the wolf.

"But, Grandma!" Little Red Riding Hood said again, "what big ears you have!"

"All the better to hear you with," growled the wolf.

Red Riding Hood began to think that something was very strange...

"But, Grandma!" she said for a third time, "what big teeth you have!"

"All the better to EAT you with!" roared the wolf, and he leapt out of bed. He reached out to grab Red Riding Hood with his long, powerful claws!

Red Riding Hood began screaming, which made her Grandma bang on the wardrobe door. The wolf roared again, not knowing that the hunter he had heard was right outside…

He kicked the door open and strode into
[cot]tage, raising his gun. He had been
[...]wolf for a long time – as that
[...]new only too well!

With one last, desperate roar, he dashed out of the cottage, determined to escape the hunter's gun for the last time. After that, he was never seen again.

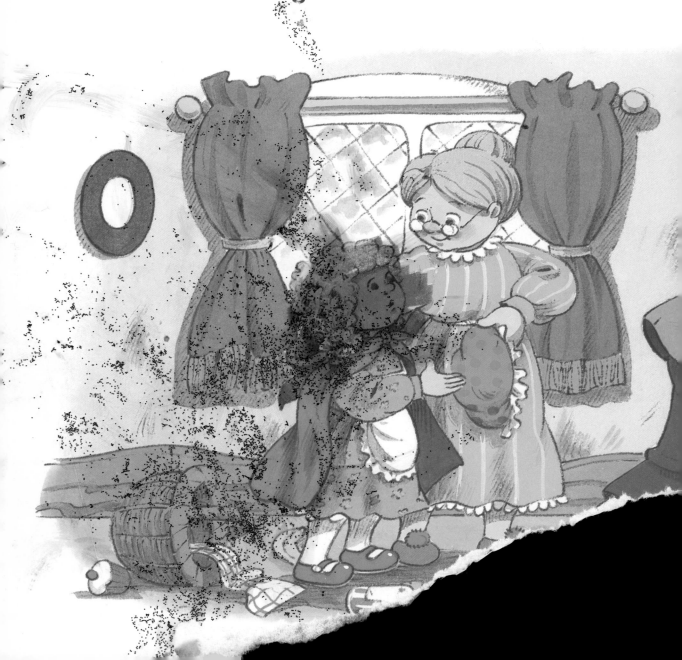